PENGUIN BOOKS

Published by the Penguin Group
Penguin Books Ltd, 27 Wrights Lane, London W8 5TZ, England
Viking Penguin, a division of Penguin Books USA Inc.
375 Hudson Street, New York, New York 10014, USA
Penguin Books Australia Ltd, Ringwood, Victoria, Australia
Penguin Books Canada Ltd, 2801 John Street, Markham, Ontario, Canada L3R 1B4
Penguin Books (NZ) Ltd, 182–190 Wairau Road, Auckland 10, New Zealand

Penguin Books Ltd, Registered Offices: Harmondsworth, Middlesex, England

First published 1990
10 9 8 7 6 5 4 3 2 1

Printed in England by Clays Ltd, St Ives plc

CONTENTS

DESIGN BY
BILLY STROBACKER
ALAN MARTIN
AND JAMIE HEWLETT

INTRODUCTION
by Peter Milligan

They couldn't get Rolf Harris, and Mel Gibson was out getting a chin-tuck when they called him, so lean lived-in Jamie Hewlett and enigmatic, endomorphic Alan Martin asked me to write this introduction instead.

I immediately began trying to figure out how to approach it. You know, an angle. Of course I enjoyed TANK GIRL it was fresh, had a wonderfully naive spontaneity, was a timely antidote to so much pompous comic rot, and so on and on and on. That was all very true and very dull. What I needed was a slant, a voice. I toyed with the idea of being humorously insulting, kicking off with something like:

"Though spasmodically spotty and by all accounts a thorough waste of time in bed, Jamie Hewlett is to comics what lead free petrol is to the ozone layer..."

But no. I quickly dumped that idea, partly because I'm just too pleasant to maintain that rude posture, but mainly because Jamie might refuse to give me back the money he owes me. It seemed I had a problem. It was getting late, the test match was rained off, those crazy creative types in the Deadline office were harassing me unmercifully for the introduction. but I still needed a slant. In desperation I considered writing it in the voice of Tank Girl, the Darling of the Outback herself. Something along the lines of,

"G'day, dickheads, any of yous seen the tinnies? I've just talked to those daggy bahhstards Martin and Hewlett and they want me to scratch together a bloody intro for this book and so I'm gonna get pisseder than a pair of pommy's pants and then..."

No, no, no, no. It just wouldn't do. I couldn't take the strine, I mean the strain, of keeping that voice up.

I could, I thought, pepper the introduction with salty anecdotes, about meetings and/or conversations I've had with the boys. That's the 'I've broken bread with the guys and I love 'em to death' school of intro writing. Let's think. Maybe the time Alan told me he found Thirtysomething mildly entertaining. Nah. Too far fetched. So how about when Jamie told me, in all seriousness, that TANK GIRL was going to take a bus from Australia to New Zealand, and was surprised when I told him that Australia was an Island? Of course, in a comic strip like TANK GIRL there's no reason why you shouldn't catch a bus, or even a tank, from Oz to Kiwiland or any other place, but I could rage on about how Hewlett's abyssmal grasp of geography is such a damning indictment of, well, of anything or anyone I particularly wanted to indict damningly.

Cry of frustration. sound of another sheet of paper crumpled into a ball. Try again, try again.

By this time I was starting to wonder whether I'd ever write this bloody introduction, and whether Hewlett and Martin would ever speak to me again. I suppose I could always go for that 'pretend you're an overread intellectual talking his philosophicals off' angle, you know....

...Of course Nietzsche tells us that the Noble Caste is always at first a barbarian, but Tank Girl, though unquestionably barbaric, is not, I feel of Good Birth, Nietzsche's prerequisite for morality. Morality? Tank Girl? Perhaps we should look at Wittgenstein....

No, perhaps we shouldn't. That old Nietzsche and co angle is just too passe, and I'm afraid the overread intellectual in me seems to have gone walkabout.

So searching for inspiration, I flipped through the pages of the first episode of Deadline, where that little minx TANK GIRL first flexed her antipodean muscles and sprung to boozy, anarchic, glorious life. There it all was: the shaven head, the kangaroos, the bush, the beer, the belly button, the tank, the girl.

But no inspiration for an introduction.

Only one thing for it, I thought. I'll have to refuse. Say I'm too busy or something.

So, I'm sorry, Jamie and Alan. I tried to write an introduction for your TANK GIRL book but it just didn't happen. I hope the book does well though; it's bloody great and deserves to sell millions.

Sincerely,

PETER MILLIGAN
Lourdes, March 1990.

TANK GIRL

KANGAROOS!

COME ON BOYS, THE BEER'S ARE ON THEM!

LET'S KICK OFF WITH A BIT OF VIOLENCE! MEET ROCKY DEADHEAD, THE HARDEST KANGAROO IN THE OUTBACK. TODAY HE'S LEADING HIS GANG OF BRAIN DEATHS ON TO ANOTHER DRUNKEN GATE CRASHING BAR-B-Q ORGY OF BLOOD'N'GUTS.

DOES ANYONE KNOW WHOSE BARBY THIS IS?

THIS IS GONNA BE A PIECE OF CAKE!

WHO CARES? SOON AS WE GET THERE WE'LL JUST KILL EVERYONE!

WOW WE JUST DON'T CARE, DO WE?

THAT'S BECAUSE WE'RE KANGAROOS........

I'M A KANGAROO!

WHAT'S A BARBY

OUR HEROINE TANKGIRL IS AFTER THE BOUNTY ON THIS FOUL MOUTHED MARSUPIAL'S HEAD!......

THINGS HAD CHANGED IN THE OUTBACK SINCE CROCODILE DUNDEE HAD MOVED TO SHOREHAM-BY-SEA. KANGAROOS HAD MOVED ON FROM DESTROYING CROPS TO SNOGGING FARMERS AND BURNING THEIR KIDS.

THE PRAIRIES OF AUSTRALIA WERE NO LONGER SAFE FOR THE HARD WORKING RED NECKS...

YOU SERIOUS? ALL THEY GOT IS HOT DOGS AND BEER BELLYS. YOU GUYS HAVE GOT ME, REMEMBER I'VE GOT A BOUNTY ON MY HEAD WORTH ONE HUNDRED THOUSAND DOLLARS I'M THAT 'ARD ME. THAT 'ARD!

HEY ROCKY, DO YOU THINK THE PEOPLE AT THIS BARBY ARE GONNA BE PACKED?

WHO THE HELL'S GONNA MESS WITH US!?........

JUST OVER THE NEXT HILL THE LOCAL POPSTARS BARBY IS IN FULL SWING!

HEY SHIRLEY YOU STUPID DUNG HEAD. WHAT HAPPENED TO THESE HOT DOGS? LOOKS LIKE YOU COOKED THEM WITH A FLAME THROWER!

AH, KEEP QUIET CRAP CAKE! I GOT MORE IMPORTANT THINGS TO DO THAN WATCH YOUR FAG HOT DOGS!

OH GEE! ARE YOU GUYS STILL BICKERING? C'MON LIGHTEN UP AND ENJOY YOURSELVES! WORSE THINGS COULD HAPPEN!..........

BOOOZ DRINK THANG!

AFTER ALL...BURNT HOT DOGS AREN'T HALF AS DEVASTATING AS KILLER KANGAROOS!.......

SUP THE BEER, SNOG THE BITCHES AND BURN THAT FAT GUY!

WE'RE NASTY AND WE SMELL!

RUN LIKE HELL FAT PEOPLE, WE'VE ALL GOT CHOCOLATE BAR'S ON OUR HEADS!

WHO INVITED THEM?

13

TANK GIRL *

THERE'S A TURNIP FOR THE BOOKS!

OK, SWEETY, CALM DOWN. WE CAN ALL IMAGINE HOW DARN EXCITED YOU MUST BE RIGHT NOW, BUT THIS IS RILLY RILLY IMPORTANT! ..... LET ME FILL YOU IN!

POW!

NOT NOW, I'M ON MY MENSTRUAL CYCLE!

WHAT HAPPENED TO THE TANK WE GAVE YOU?!

WHAT THE FOOOSH ARE YOU ON ABOUT?!

NEVER MIND! HERE'S THE MISSION; THERE'S GONNA BE A BIG PARTY IN SIDNEY HARBOUR AT 4.30 TH'S AFTERNOON. ALL THE WORLD'S BIGGEST TRADE DELEGATES WILL BE THERE!

PRESIDENT HOGAN WILL BE HOSTING THE DO. AS I'M SURE YOU KNOW, IT WAS THE PRE-SIDENT'S NINETY SECOND BIRTHDAY LAST WEEK. THE POOR GUY'S GETTING ON, AND HAS TERRIBLE TROU-BLE WITH HIS BOWELS!

HE HE

WE WANT YOU TO DELIVER A CONSIGNMENT OF COLOSTOMY BAG'S TO THE PRESIDENT BEFORE HE DROPS HIS LOAD!

RUMBLE

OOPS!

HA HA HAHA HA H HA

I'M SURE YOU CAN IMAGINE THE IMPORTANCE OF THIS MISSION .... CAN YOU DO IT?

NO SWEAT!

BAD

YOWZA!

AND REMEMBER, TANK GIRL, NO MESSING UP!

PRESIDENT HOGAN'S THE ONE WHOSE GON-NA MESS UP. AH HA HA HA!

VOOOSHH!

AND BE ON THE LOOKOUT FOR X WAR CRIMS!

TALY HO TRUSTY TANK THANG!

CLAN CL*AM CHUG

OOPS ALMOST FORGOT- SIDNEY'S THIS A WAY!

TANK

THE FIRE OF LURVE BURNS DEEPLY IN MY ROTTING HEART. MY LOVE FOR THIS CREATURE OF BEAUTY RUNS DEEP IN MY TWISTED VEINS. MY EARS ARE GIVEN LIFE AT THE MENTION OF HER NAME, AND MY ONLY MEMORY OF THE BLONDE BEAUTY IS THAT FATAL THREAT BISTOWED ON HER BY HER VICIOUS GRANNY!

WAR CRIM! ME!

MR BISHOP IS VERY PUNCTUAL, JANE!

SO DON'T BE LATE FOR DINNER!

JANE!

JANE, I'M COMING JANE

JANE!

JANE!

COULD DO WITH A GOOD SHAVE!

I'M HERE!

THUD!

WHERE'S JANE, PUGFACE?

WHAT THE FOOSH!?

18

AND THE MERCY SEAT IS WAITING!

POW!

SPLAMBO!

BUG OFF, PUG FACE!

OOOF

IN THE COMMOTION TANK GIRL GRABS THE NEAREST THING!

ARHH!

SUCK THIS

ALAS DEAR YORICK- I KNEW HIS SHELF!

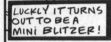

LUCKLY IT TURNS OUT TO BE A MINI BLITZER!

DOOOSH!

ONCE AGAIN TANK GIRL LANDS ON HER BONCE, THIS TIME KNOCKING HER SELF OUT.

YOW OOOF! CRUNCH!!!

BAD

UNTIL NEXTDAY!

SHEESH! YOU'RE LOOKING A MESS, TANK GIRL. WHAT HAPPENED?

SURE IS!

CHRIST KNOWS. CAN'T REMEMBER A THING THAT'S HAPPENED IN THE LAST TWO DAYS!

LOOKS LIKE WE BOTH MESSED UP!

GUESS THAT MEANS YOU DON'T KNOW YOUR FACE IS ALL OVER THE PAPERS?

SOUNDS LIKE FAME! (AGAIN)

YLY NEWSPAPER $

DUMP **MASTER**

PRESIDENT DROPS HIS LOAD!

TANK GIRL TO BLAME!

☆ JAMIE (TANKBOY) 88 ©

NEXT TIME: THE SACK!?

TANK

AND SO OUR STORY BEGINS.

VEX GODGLOVE THE NOTORIOUS BACK STABBING, LOW-LIFE, BOUNTY HUNTER, FAKES A NASTY ACCIDENT DEEP IN THE HEART OF THE OUTBACK!

YESIREEEE! AN'THIS TIME NEXT WEEK I'LL BE DRIVING AROUND IN A 5 GEAR, METALLIC, CONVERTABLE, MUSTANG WITH MATCHING MUDGUARDS!

I WAS BORN UNDER A STATIONARY CAR A CHROME LADEN STATIONARY DODGE!

AND I'LL BUY IT WITH THE REWARD MONEY I GET FOR THE CAPTURE OF THAT LITTLE TART, TANK GIRL!

BOY O BOY THIS IS GONNA BE THE EASIEST MILLION I'LL EVER MAKE!

AS ALWAYS VEX HAS A CUNNING PLAN!

I'LL JUST SIT TIGHT UNTIL THE DUMB BITCH ARRIVES AND STICKS HER NOSE IN,

LIKE THEY INEVITABLY DO!

CHINK!

RECKON I'LL START BY BREAKING HER LEGS!, THEN I'LL STOMP UP AND DOWN ON HER BACK-BONE!..

SHE'S JUST A WEAK PATHETIC WOMAN, SHE'S NO MATCH FOR THE AWSOME MULTITUDE'S OF VEX GOD...

UH?!

UNTIL IT SNAP'S INTO TINY, LITTLE PIECE'S!

AFTER ALL...

22

23

GUNS OF BECKTON!

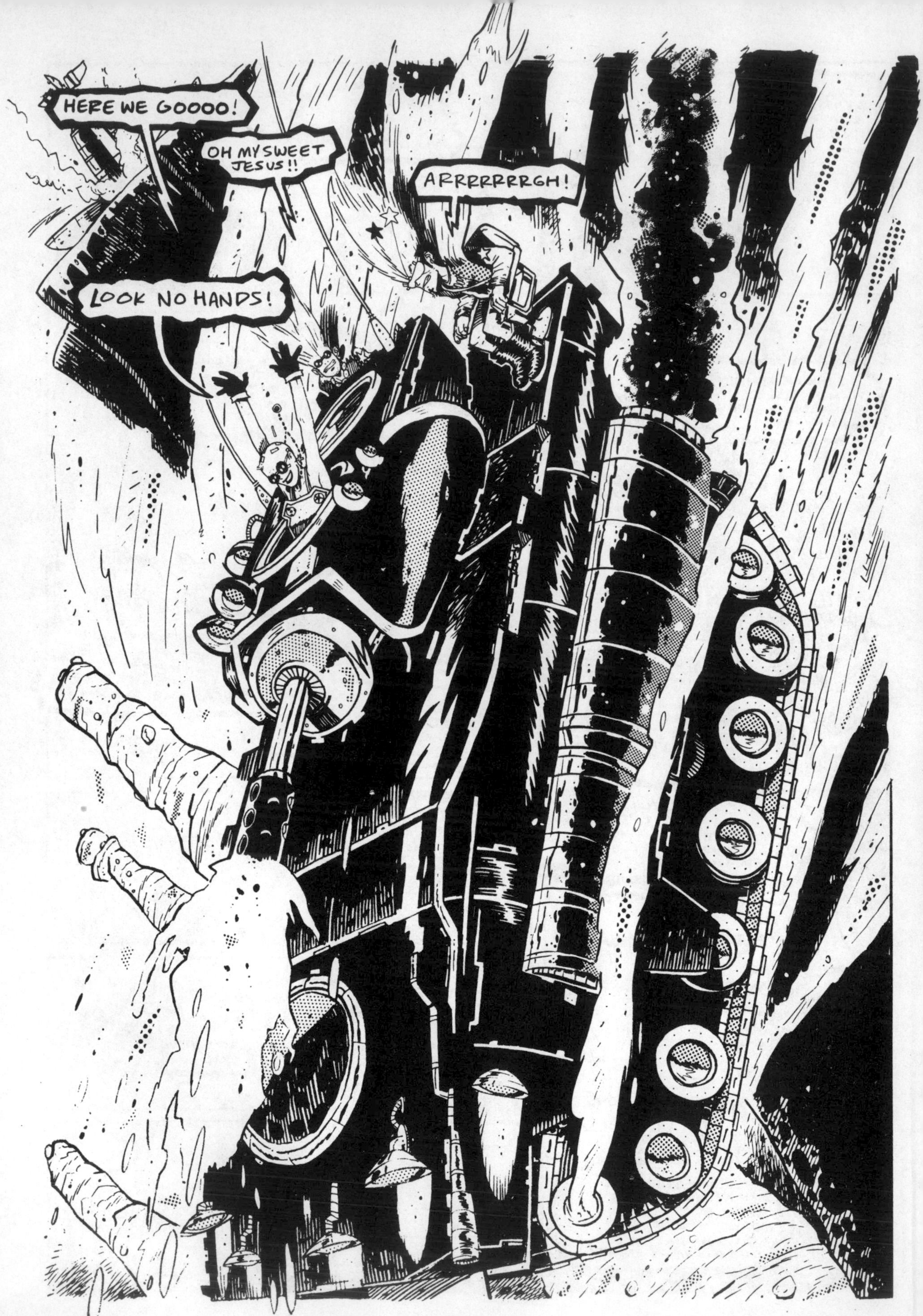
HERE WE GOOOO!
OH MY SWEET JESUS!!
ARRRRRRRGH!
LOOK NO HANDS!

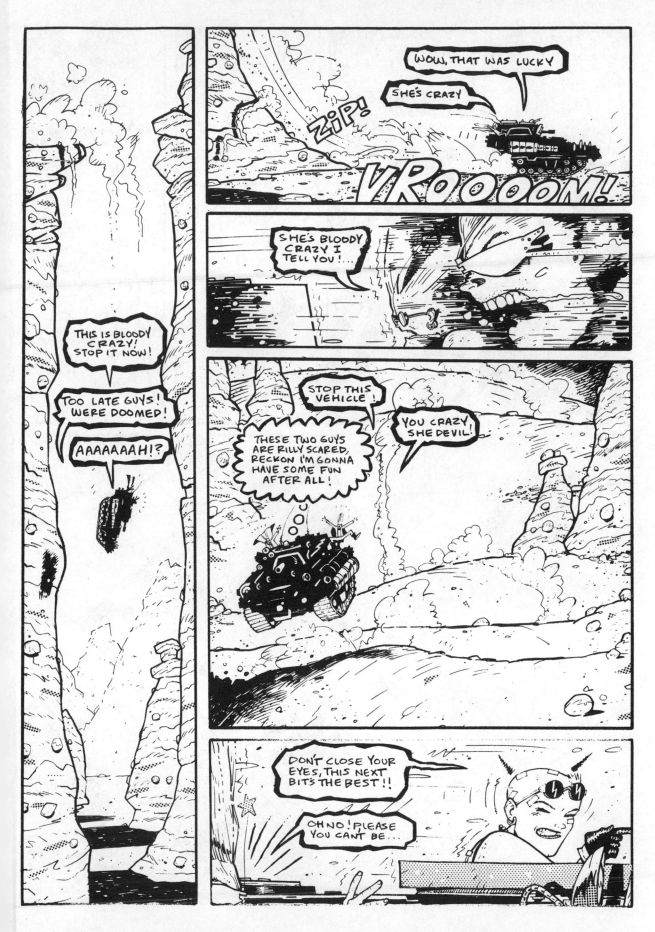

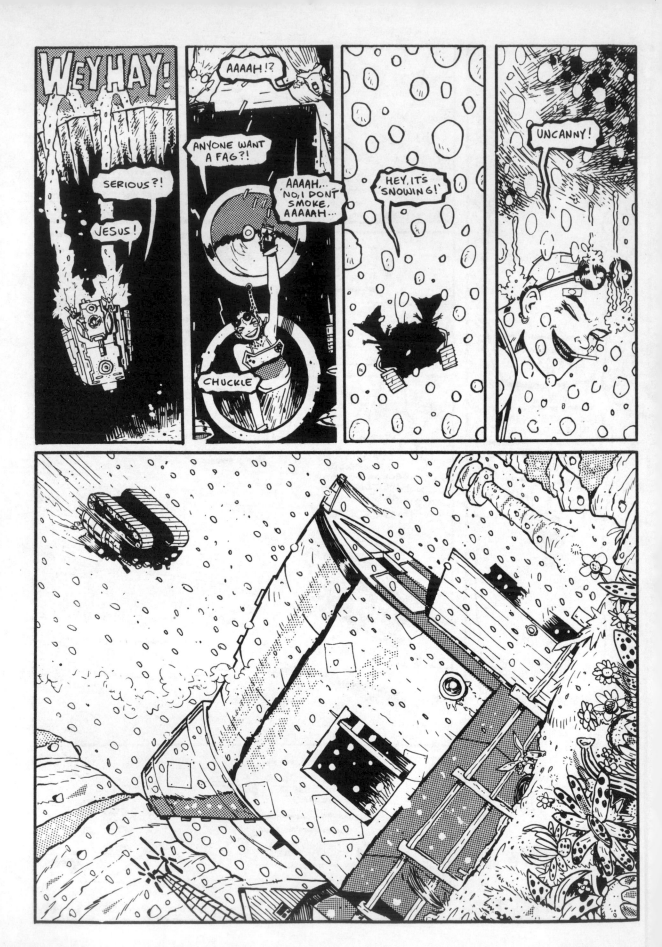

How to draw Tank Girl the Jamie way

THAT'S ME

1 PENCIL IN A NUDE FIGURE WITH AN HB PENCIL ENSURING THE PROPORTIONS ARE CORRECT ....

2 ... ADD THE APPROPRIATE CLOTHES, BOOTS, T-SHIRT, HAT AND PANTIES ....

3 ... THEN INK THE BASTARD! ....

THE TOMORROW PEOPLE

YOU! IN THE SHACK! THIS WILL BE YOUR ONLY WARNING! COME OUT WITH YOUR HANDS UP BY THE COUNT OF TEN, OTHERWISE THERE WILL BE.... TROUBLE!....

THERE'S GONNA BE SHOOTIN!

BANG BANG

BOOGY BOOGY BOOGY!

HONKEY

RIP OFF

HOLY SMOKING, THERE'S LOTS OF REALLY NASTY LOOK-ING PEOPLE STANDING OUT FRONT, AND THEY'VE GOT THIS MASSIVE TANK AND LOTS OF BIG GUNS!

MUST BE FOR ME!

DON'T PANIC, KIDS, I'VE GOT A SECRET TRAP DOOR IN THE BACK ROOM, IT LEADS TO A MOUND OF ROCKS BEHIND THE SHACK. WE CAN MAKE A CLEAN GET AWAY, ...IT'S THE LEAST I CAN DO FOR YOU AFTER MESSING UP YOUR PRETTY LITTLE FACE!

GREAT! LET'S GO BOYS!

YOUR TIMES UP, DIRTBAGS, ARE YOU COMING OUT, OR DO WE HAVE TO BLAST OUR WAY IN?

IM5

WHAT'S THE MATTER, STEVIE? YOU TANNED YOUR PANTS?

COME ON UNCLE, GET A MOVE ON!! OOH IT'S DARK!

WHAT EVER HAPPENED TO LADIES FIRST?

HEY! I FOUND MY OLD DAME EDNA MOULDS.

ALAS, THE AFTER EFFECTS OF DRED'S VOODOO MAGIC STRIKE AT THE MOST UNCOMPROMIZING MOMENTS.....

OH NO! YOU AND YOUR POXY PLASTIC SURGERY CRAP, STEVIE, I CAN'T FIT DOWN THE BLOODY HOLE!

DON'T PANIC, THE AFTER EFFECTS ONLY LAST A COUPLE OF HOURS!

SORRY TANK GIRL!

OH GREAT! WHAT AM I SUPPOSE TO DO IN THE MEANTIME!?

TRY SURRENDERING! MAYBE THEY WON'T RECOGNIZE YOU!

"SIZE OF A WATER BUFFALO"

AND SO...

HI GUYS, YOU MUST BE LOOKING FOR TANK GIRL, SHE'S IN THE BACK ROOM POWDERING HER NOSE, FEEL FREE TO GO IN AND ROUGH HER UP AS MUCH AS YOU LIKE!...

40

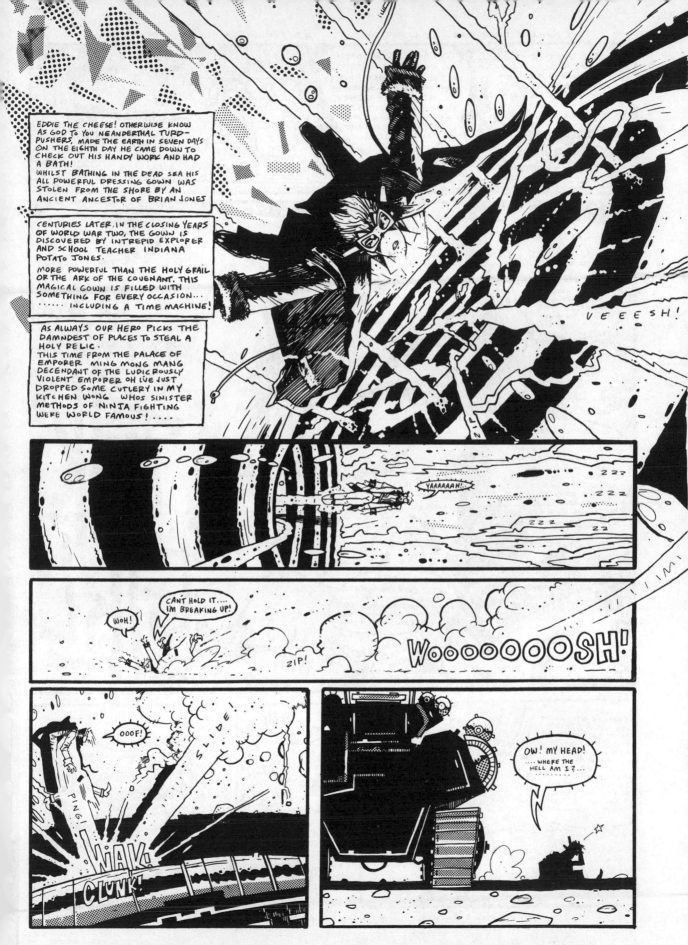

EDDIE THE CHEESE! OTHERWISE KNOW AS GOD TO YOU NEANDERTHAL TURD-PUSHERS, MADE THE EARTH IN SEVEN DAYS ON THE EIGHTH DAY HE CAME DOWN TO CHECK OUT HIS HANDY WORK AND HAD A BATH!
WHILST BATHING IN THE DEAD SEA HIS ALL POWERFUL DRESSING GOWN WAS STOLEN FROM THE SHORE BY AN ANCIENT ANCESTOR OF BRIAN JONES

CENTURIES LATER, IN THE CLOSING YEARS OF WORLD WAR TWO, THE GOWN IS DISCOVERED BY INTREPID EXPLORER AND SCHOOL TEACHER INDIANA POTATO JONES.
MORE POWERFUL THAN THE HOLY GRAIL OR THE ARK OF THE COVENANT, THIS MAGICAL GOWN IS FILLED WITH SOMETHING FOR EVERY OCCASION...
...... INCLUDING A TIME MACHINE!

AS ALWAYS OUR HERO PICKS THE DAMNDEST OF PLACES TO STEAL A HOLY RELIC.
THIS TIME FROM THE PALACE OF EMPEROR MING MONG MANG DECENDANT OF THE LUDICROUSLY VIOLENT EMPEROR OH I'VE JUST DROPPED SOME CUTLERY IN MY KITCHEN WONG, WHOS SINISTER METHODS OF NINJA FIGHTING WERE WORLD FAMOUS! ....

VEEESH!

YAAAAAAH!

ZZZ
ZZZ
ZZZ
ZZ

WOH!

CAN'T HOLD IT....
I'M BREAKING UP!

ZIP!

WOOOOOOOOSH!

OOOF!

SLIDE!

PING!

WAK!

CLUNK!

OW! MY HEAD!
.... WHERE THE HELL AM I?...

45

MEANWHILE, THE AIR LANES AND SEA LANES EMPTY TO CLEAR THE APPROACH TO SURFERS PARADISE.... A THUNDERING ROAR OF STATE OF THE ART TURBO ENGINES AND THE ACIDIC STENCH OF HIGH OCTANE FUEL AND PINK PARAFFIN HERALD THE ARRIVAL OF TANK GIRL'S BOSOM BUDDIES

JET GIRL!

SUBGIRL!

G'DAY DOG'S BREASTS! BIN HERE LONG?

ABOUT HALF AN HOUR, YOU OLD TOSSER. WHERE HAVE YOU BEEN?!

GOT STUCK IN THE SLOW LANE!..GOD I HATE YOU!

OH, BY THE WAY, I GOT THE CAKE!

JESUS!

PPY BiRTH

I GOT A PRESENT FOR TANK GIRL AND I PUT YOUR NAME IN THE CARD, OK?! IT'S A VERY FUNNY CARD AND THE PRESENT'S QUITE NICE AS WELL!..

OK!?

DID YOU GET HER A PRESENT? I FORGOT!

OH SCREW THIS ULTRA BANAL CONVERSATION DUMB ASS HIPPY!

C'MON BULLET BRAIN, LET'S GO!

AND SO SUBGIRL AND JET GIRL SET OFF FOR SURFERS PARADISE WHERE THE WAVES ARE HIGH AND THE SAND IS GOLDEN AND WHERE YOUNG STEVIE PLANS TO STAGE TANK GIRL'S BIRTHDAY CELEBRATIONS...

OH YEAH, I GOT THE CAKE

ARRGH

SCRIPT—ALAN + JAMIE ★ ART—JAMIE ★ LETTERS—ALAN ★ THIS ONE FOR MEL + GLYN ★ STUNT CO-ORDINATOR—MICHAEL

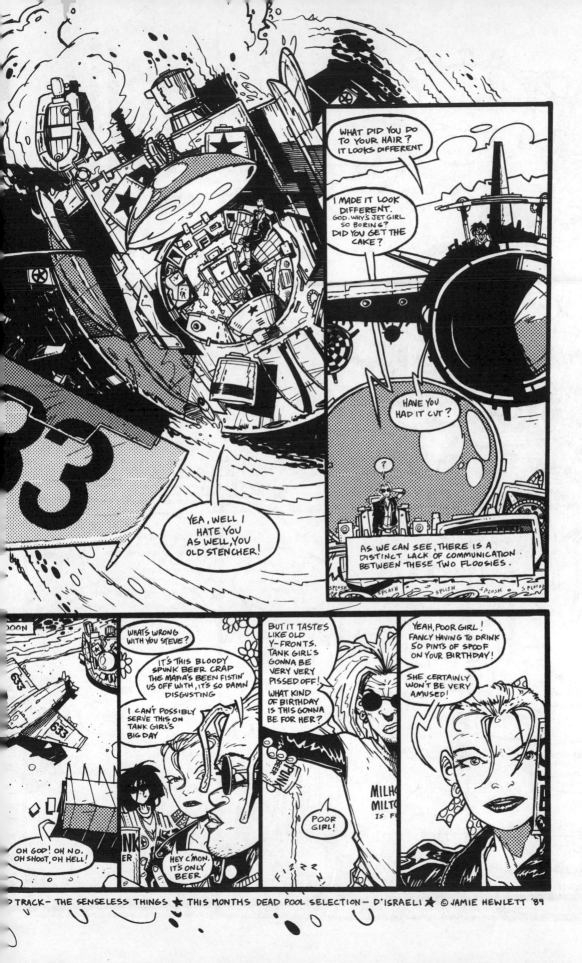

HAPPY BIRTHDAY

I'M NOT AMUSED!

YIKES!

OOPS

ARGH!

SPUNK BEER

TANK GIRL*

IN

THE AUSTRALIAN JOB Part ONE

Co-STARRING: JETGIRL 'N' SUBGIRL

THIS IS A BLOODY OUTRAGE, IT'S THE WORST BIRTHDAY I'VE EVER HAD!

SHE'S MAD, SHE IS MAD!

DO YOU THINK SHE'LL DO SOMETHING STUPID?

DIDN'T SHE LIKE THE CAKE?

CASTLE XXX DECENT BEER

S.U.L.K!

STEVIE, WHAT HAPPENED TO ALL THE REAL DECENT BEERS?

WELL, RUMOUR HAS IT THAT IT'S BEING HOARDED AWAY BY THE AUSTRALIAN MAFIA, SOMEWHERE IN SYDNEY.

SYDNEY, EH? I THINK IT'S TIME WE WENT TO SEE MR. BRIDGER THE ABO!

YOU MEAN THE MR. BRIDGER, THE ULTIMATE MASTERMIND OF ORGANISED CRIME. WHY DO WE WANT TO GO SEE HIM?

BECAUSE HE'S GOT A BIG NOB! ...WHY DO YOU THINK WE'RE GONNA SEE HIM, STUPID? WE'RE GONNA DO A JOB, A HEIST, THE BIGGEST, HUGEST, NASTIEST SWEAT-RIDDEN BEER HEIST IN THE HISTORY OF BREWING!

CHUCKLE!

OH!

LATER AT MR.BRIDGER'S...

IT'S NICE TO SEE YOU AGAIN TANK GIRL, WHAT CAN I DO FOR YOU?

NICE TO SEE YOU TOO MR BRIDGER... I'VE GOT A JOB LINED UP A BIG JOB.. B.I.G. BIG!

OH, I SEE, WELL THE BOGS OUT THE BACK, SORRY BUT THERE'S NO LOO PAPER!

NO, NO, I'M TALKING ABOUT A HEIST, A ROBBERY, A JOB!

OH A JOB, I THOUGHT YOU MEANT A JOBBY JOBBY PLOP PLOP, HA HA, CHUCKLE. SILLY ME. WELL, YOU'D BETTER TELL ME ALL ABOUT IT!

EVERY FRIDAY AT NOON THE MAFIA MOVES A SHIPMENT OF STOLEN BEER THROUGH SYDNEY. MY PLAN IS TO HOLD-UP THE TRUCK AND STEAL THE BLOODY LOT... THEN MAKE IT TO THE OUTBACK BEFORE THEY KNOW WHAT'S HIT THEM!...

WHERE DO I FIT INTO THIS PLAN?

WELL MR.B, WE'RE GONNA NEED SOME VERY SPECIAL EQUIPMENT THAT ONLY YOU CAN SUPPLY!

ONE HOUR LATER..

IT'S GONNA BE A VERY DIFFICULT JOB, AND THE ONLY WAY TO GET THROUGH IT IS TO DO IT AS A TEAM! ·······

NOW, THIS IS THE PLAN—

THE PLAN
BEER
US!
YUM YUM
PISSED!

FINALLY AND VERY QUICKLY I WOULD LIKE TO INTRODUCE THE LADS WHO ARE GONNA BE DOING THE JOB WITH ME—

JET GIRL 'N' SUBGIRL, THEY MAY LOOK STUPID BUT THESE TWO CHINLESS WONDERS WILL GET YOU OUT OF SYDNEY FASTER THAN ANYTHING ON FOUR WHEELS,

BOOGA, STEVIE, CAMP KOALA WILL BE RIDING IN THE RED TANK WITH SUBGIRL,

MR PRECOCIOUS WILL BE RIDING SHOT GUN WITH JET GIRL IN THE WHITE TANK, AND AS ALWAYS THE SQUEEKY TOY RAT WILL BE RIDING WITH ME IN THE BLUE TANK.

I WILL NOT WORK WITH AMATEURS

SHOTGUN

SCOOBY

WELL DONE BUSH, YOU'VE ONLY BEEN IN TWO MINUTES AND YOU'RE CAUSING TROUBLE ALREADY.

YOU ALL KNOW BEN GREEN, HE'S JUST FINISHED TWO YEARS IN CELL BLOCK H. HE'S AS HONEST AS THE DAY IS LONG AND YOU CAN TRUST HIM. HE'LL BE STANDING BY WITH TWO FAST TANKS IN CASE ANYTHING GOES WRONG. HE'S GOT SOME FUNNY HABITS, BUT MAKE HIM WELCOME.

THIS IS MR BRIDGER, WHO'LL BE FUNDING THE JOB, HE'S VERY IMPORTANT TO THE OPERATION, SO SHOW HIM SOME RESPECT

FUNNY?

WIRE WOOL WORLD

RIGHT, THAT'S IT, ANY QUESTIONS?

AND SO, OVER THE NEXT FEW DAYS, STEVIE, BOOGA, MR BRIDGER, BEN AND THE GIRLS PLAN THE BIGGEST BEER HEIST IN HISTORY, 2000 TONS OF LAGER THROUGH SYDNEY IN A TRAFFIC JAM...... BRILLIANT!

YAARGH! BOMBS AWAY!

NEAT!

TANK GIRL YOU'RE ONLY SUPPOSED TO BLOW THE BLOODY DOORS OFF!

VVROOOM

WHAT HAPPENED TO ALL THE PRECISION PLANNING?

VROOM!

AMY JOHNSON

THURSDAY 12.15 SYDNEY

RIGHT, THIS IS IT, EVERYONE GET INTO POSITION, THE TRUCK WILL BE THERE IN HALF AN HOUR!

WHY DO YOU KEEP TALKING LIKE MICHAEL CAINE, TANK GIRL?

WHAT? SHU-UP, LEAVE IT OUT WHY DON'T YA!

BLOODY 'ELL!

WHO'S MICHAEL CAINE?

DROP DEAD JET GIRL!

12.45 THE TRUCK LOAD OF BEER MOVES OFF, RIGHT ON SCHEDULE

SO I PUSHED WIRE COAT HANGERS THROUGH HIS FEET AND KNITTING NEEDLES THROUGH HIS FACE, AND STILL HE WOULDN'T TALK...

OF COURSE I'M NOT WEARING ANY UNDERWEAR..

LAGER FOS

TAKE IT EASY DRIVER 8!

SURE THING BOSS

I JUST PULLED OUT MY CHOPPER AND WIZZED ALL OVER THE ROOTS OF COMICS

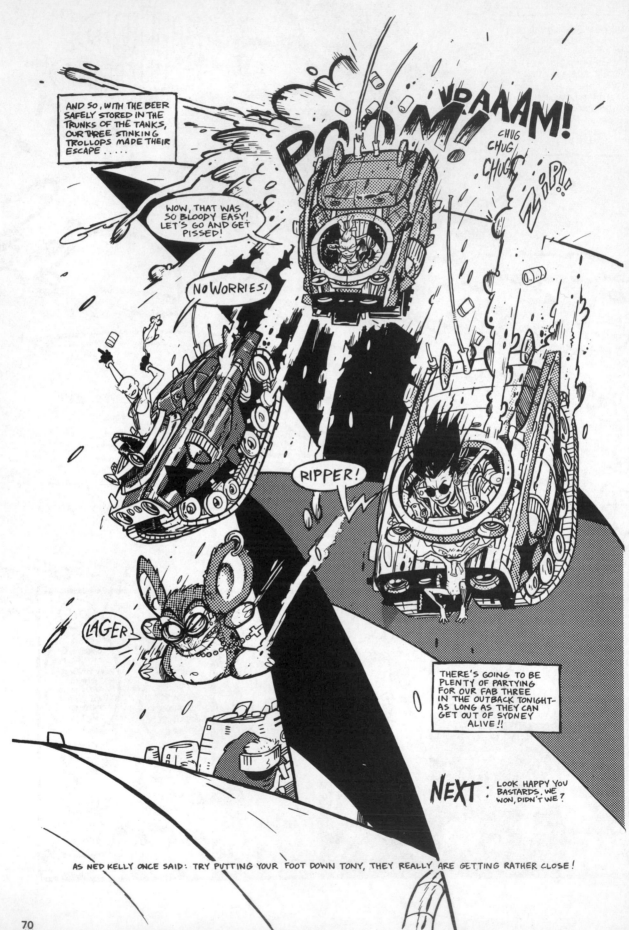

ALL THESE SPEED SHOTS COULD LEAD TO LOTS OF NEEDLESSLY MESSY ACCIDENTS, ESPECIALLY FOR THE CLUELESS COMIC REVIEWERS FROM FANTASY Y-FRONTS ADVERTISER ON THEIR WAY TO THE ANNUAL TOSSER'S CONVENTION...

QUICK, DOWN THE MAIN SEWER!

GOD, WHAT A STENCH!

THOSE DAMN POLICE ARE STILL ON OUR TAIL!

LEAVE THIS TO ME

TOUR BUS★

SKREEEECH!

LOOK OUT!

CHRIST!

MOVE OVER DOPEY!

AS THE CHASE REACHES FEVER PITCH, TANK GIRL IS SO WOUND UP WITH EXCITEMENT THAT SHE LETS RIP WITH ONE OF HER FAVORITE TOYS....

LIMPET MINES!

BREAKING THE SOUND BARRIER

KA POOM A!

AND THE QUARTER BACK IS TOAST!

AND THEN STRAIGHT ONTO THE FREEWAY FOR THE RENDEZVOUS WITH THE BIG TANK..

GET THE WHEELS IN LINE, GET THE WHEELS IN LINE!...

C'MON

ND MONEY AND FLOWERS TO YOUR LOCAL HUNT SABOTEUR

SOOOON THE TANKS ARE SAFELY ONBOARD AND THE FRANTIC GANG SET ABOUT UNLOADING THE BEER....

YAARHOOOO! WE DONE IT, WE BLOODY WELL DONE IT!

HELP US UNLOAD THE STUFF SO WE CAN DITCH THE TANKS!

SOON IN THE MOUNTAINS...

THERE THEY GO!

GEEE WHAT A WASTE!

SHOOM! KABAM! DOOSH

SPLIT OPEN SOME TUBES BEN

YUM YUM

DID YOU GET ANY SHERRY?

MEANWHILE IN EARTH'S ORBIT OUR ALIEN PALS DISCOVER THE FOUL ARSE HOLE LIKE TASTE OF BEEF BURGERS AND DECIDE TO JETISON THE FESTERING MAC BEFORE IT RUINS THEIR CLEAN COMPLEXIONS AND DESTROYS THEIR OVER-FOLIATED PLANET.........

CRAP

''PING''

LOOK OUT BURGER!

PING!

SWERVE! SWERVE! SWERVE!

SWERVE

HOLY SHIT. WE'RE BALANCING ON THE EDGE!

NOBODY MOVE AND NOBODY GET OUT EITHER, OTHERWISE WE'LL ALL GO OVER!

TANK GIRL*

SOME TIMES WHEN I'M ASLEEP I DREAM THAT I CAN FLY. IT'S NOT REALLY FLYING, SOMETIMES I DREAM THAT I'M RUNNING AWAY FROM THE ARMY DOWN PAST THE PUB NEAR STEVIE'S HOUSE.... AND I START LEAPING, OVER ROCKS AND BUSHES ..... AND THEN I FEEL MY HEART KIND OF TUGGING UPWARDS AND I PUT MY ARMS OUT LIKE WINGS.... AND RAISE MY LEGS UP TO MY CHEST LIKE UNDERCARRIAGE ....THEN I JUST GLIDE ALONG... LEAVING THE ARMY BEHIND ME... GOD I'M F*CKED......

ONE THING THAT HAS ALWAYS DISTUR-
BED ME IS THE FACT THAT PEOPLE
HAVE TWO SETS OF CLOTHES — A SCRUFFY
SET FOR MUCKING ABOUT IN AND
A SMART SET FOR GOING OUT IN.
I MEAN, DO YOU CHANGE INTO A
DIFFERENT PERSON WHEN YOU GO
SOMEWHERE 'SPECIAL'? NO! YOU'RE
STILL THE SAME BUMHOLE YOU WERE
BUILDING THAT TREE HOUSE THIS
MORNING. SO WHY DRESS DIFFERENT?
ARE WE LIVING IN THE MIDDLE AGES?
ARE YOU ALL SUCKERS FOR THAT
SOPHISTICATION CRAP THEY PUMP
OUT ON T.V.?

OR DO YOU LICK THE BOOTS OF THOSE
BIG MEN TYPE WANKERS WITH
LOTS OF CASH?
   IF THERE'S ONE THING I CAN'T STAND
IT'S VANITY, ESPECIALLY IN BLOKES.

   I LOVE MY CLOTHES.

THIS MAY SOUND STRANGE, BUT I CAN TELL WHEN IT'S GOING TO RAIN....
REALLY! I'M FEELING VERY ODD OF LATE, I'VE BEEN ACTING VERY
ODD TOO, TALKING TO MYSELF, GRINNING AND LAUGHING FOR NO REASON.
SOME THING'S GOING ON. MY LIFE SEEMS TO BE COMING TOGETHER, TAKING
SOME REAL DIRECTION. THIS JUST WON'T DO ...
THE TIMES THEY ARE A CHANGIN.

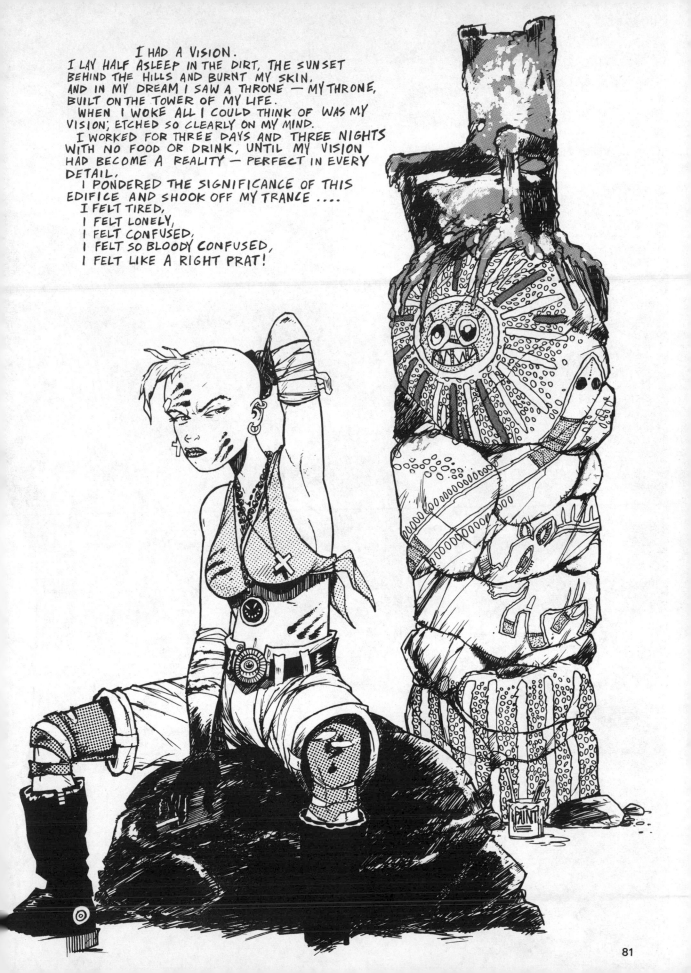

I HAD A VISION.
I LAY HALF ASLEEP IN THE DIRT, THE SUNSET
BEHIND THE HILLS AND BURNT MY SKIN,
AND IN MY DREAM I SAW A THRONE — MY THRONE,
BUILT ON THE TOWER OF MY LIFE.
   WHEN I WOKE ALL I COULD THINK OF WAS MY
VISION; ETCHED SO CLEARLY ON MY MIND.
   I WORKED FOR THREE DAYS AND THREE NIGHTS
WITH NO FOOD OR DRINK, UNTIL MY VISION
HAD BECOME A REALITY — PERFECT IN EVERY
DETAIL.
   I PONDERED THE SIGNIFICANCE OF THIS
EDIFICE AND SHOOK OFF MY TRANCE ....
   I FELT TIRED,
   I FELT LONELY,
   I FELT CONFUSED,
   I FELT SO BLOODY CONFUSED,
   I FELT LIKE A RIGHT PRAT!

SCREEEEPT ★ JAMIE  DRAWIN'S ★ JAMIE   LETTERS ★ ALAN   SOUND TRACK ★ NO. 10, UPPING ST.

87

ENTER LUCA TAVALIERI. HE WAS THE DON OF THE BOXING MAFIA, A CROSS BETWEEN SCARFACE AND ORSON WELLS. I WAS GOING TO BE FIGHTING HIS GOLDEN BOY, A BIG BLACK KANGAROO BY THE NAME OF KLUTCH.

OH SHOOT TANK GIRL, IT'S THE DON! WHAT DO WE DO NOW?

SHUT YOUR NECK AND MAKE LIKE YOU'RE AN ANIMAL!

SO DIS IS THA BIG BAD MISSILE SPITTING SON OF A BITCH I'VE HEARD SO MUCH ABOUT!

HA HAR!

SPARTA

SPARTAN

YOU KNOW THE WORD OUT ON THE STREET IS THAT YOUR BOY'Z GONNA KILL MY BOY!? IS DAT SO?

DON'T YOU GIVE ME ALL THAT MAFIA RESPECT CRAP, YOU FAT SCROTUM! TELL US WHAT YOU WANT THEN PISS OFF! WE'RE BUSY TRAINING

TANKGIRL AND LUCA TAVALIRI WASTED ABOUT AN HOUR CALLING EACH OTHER NAMES AND ARGUING..... EVENTUALLY THEY RAN OUT OF THINGS TO CALL EACH OTHER, SO LUCA CAME TO THE POINT...

OK BITCH DOG! HERE'S THE SCORE, I'VE GOT A LOT OF MONEY RIDING ON MY BOY TO WIN THIS FIGHT BY THE THIRD ROUND! I'M TALKIN' KNOCKOUT! YOUR BOY'S GONNA TAKE A FALL IN THE THIRD ROUND OTHER WISE THE BOTH OF YOU'S IS GONNA BE PROPIN' UP A MOTORWAY!

YOU BET FAT BOY!

HEY, WATCH THE MOUTH LITTLE LADY! I'LL BREAK YOUR FACE IF YOU SPEAK TO ME LIKE THAT! YOU NO GOOD PIECE OF CRAP!

CRIPES?

YOU'RE LOOKING AT CONCRETE SLIPPERS YOU BITCH!

GET MY DRIFT?!

88

IT WAS AT THIS POINT THAT TANK GIRL WENT CRAZY AND LEPT ON LUCA.....

SON OF A FAT BITCH!

YAR?

TANK GIRL?

HEY BACK OFF!

THREE BLACK EYES, 2 BUSTED LIPS AND A TORN SILK SUIT LATER, TANK GIRL DECIDED TO NEGOTIATE....

SPANNA

OK, YOU FAT SLUG-PIMP HOOD-DOG FACED ASS HOLE, MY BOY WILL TAKE THE DIVE FOR FIVE GRAND. NO MORE, NO LESS!

FIVE GRAND!?

LUCA TAVELIERI BEGAN TO SWEAT. HE LOOKED WORRIED. HE MUST HAVE BET A HELL OF A LOT OF MONEY ON HIS BOY WINNING IN THE THIRD ROUND, HE OBVIOUSLY DIDN'T BET ON TANK GIRL BEING SUCH AN ARROGANT BITCH. HE HAD NO CHOICE BUT TO GIVE US THE FIVE GRAND, HE'D OBVIOUSLY BELIEVED ALL THE LIES AND RUMOURS ABOUT ME BEING THE HARDEST BOXER IN THE UNIVERSE, AND HE KNEW TANK GIRL WASN'T AFRAID OF HIS DULL UNORIGINAL DEATH THREATS!

AND SO MUCH TO HIS DISLIKE, LUCA AGREED TO THE FIVE GRAND....

OK BITCH, YOU GOT A DEAL!

THAT'S CASH! UPFRONT BEFORE THE FIGHT DORK!

THIS IS CRAZY TANK GIRL! NO WAY AM I GONNA LAST UNTIL THE THIRD ROUND!

SPA

OF COURSE YOU WON'T. I KNEW THAT ALL ALONG

AND SO THE NIGHT OF THE BIG FIGHT CREPT UP LIKE A BOIL ON MY BACK SIDE, THE STALLS WERE ALL FULL OF HOODS AND GEEKS. THERE WERE EVEN SOME FAMOUS FACES IN THE CROWD, THEY'D ALL COME TO SEE ME FIGHT AND THEY HAD ALL BET BIG BUCKS ON ME...

AND THEY WERE ALL GONNA LOOSE!

WELCOME LADIES AND GENTS, TO THE FIGHT THAT WILL END ALL FIGHTS! IN THE BLUE CORNER, ABDUL KLUTCH 68 FIGHTS UNDEFEATED AND IN THE RED CORNER, THE NEW BOXING SENSATION, BIG BOOGA BALL BREAKER! NO FIGHTS TO DATE! BUT WHAT A REPUTATION!

KETTLE HEAD

IT WAS LONG AGO WHEN THE WHITE MEN TRIED FOR THE LAST TIME TO TAKE THIS SACRED GROUND FROM US, I WAS A SMALL CHILD, ABOUT YOUR AGE ......

THE TRIBAL ELDERS COULD SENSE THE TROUBLE BREWING, BUT THEY DID NOTHING....

THEY SOME HOW KNEW THE SPIRITS OF THE EARTH WOULD TAKE CARE OF THE PROBLEM...

WE HAD NEVER HAD A QUARREL WITH THESE WHITE MEN BEFORE, BUT FOR A REASON UNKNOWN TO US THEY HAD AN INTENSE HATRED FOR ALL OUR RACE....

RIGHT. LISTEN UP YOU ARSE FACED SCUM BAGS!

HISS   YER   BOD   SCUM   ?

WOF

WE'VE HAD ENOUGH OF YOU FILTHY BASTARDS SMELLING UP THE LAND AND SCARING OUR KIDS WE WANT YOU OFF THIS LAND SO WE CAN DO SOMETHING USEFUL WITH IT!...

BUT THIS IS THE ONLY LAND WE HAVE LEFT, WHERE WILL WE GO?

YOU'RE NOMADS AREN'T YOU?

SO JUST PISS OFF!

AND WHAT DO WE HAVE HERE? YOU'RE A SEXY YOUNG THING AREN'T YOU?!

THE FATHER OF THESE MEN SEEMED TO TAKE A SHINE TO MY ELDER SISTER...

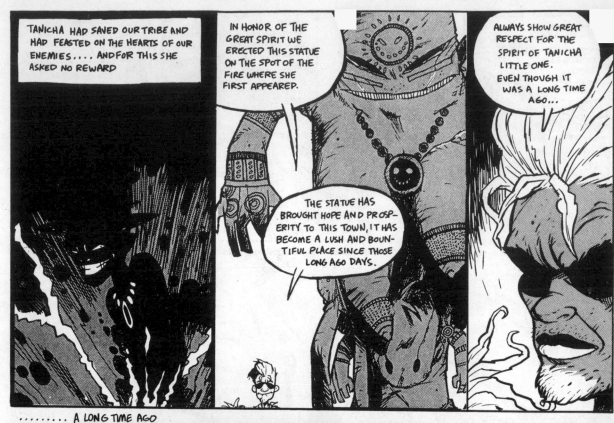

.... A LONG TIME AGO

THE BLOODY END

THE PREPOSTEROUS BOLLOX OF THE SITUATION

DEAR MOM,

I KNOW IT'S BEEN A LONG TIME SINCE I LAST WROTE TO YOU, BUT THINGS HAVE BEEN GETTING RATHER HECTIC.

I'M ALRIGHT THOUGH. I'M TAKING REAL GOOD CARE OF MYSELF.

I'VE GOT A FEW THINGS TO TELL YOU ABOUT, SO I'LL START WITH THE GOSSIP FIRST...

I HAVEN'T SEEN MUCH OF STEVIE LATELY (YOU REMEMBER STEVIE, HE WAS THE ONE WHO DRANK ALL OF YOUR CHRISTMAS SHERRY AND CLOGGED UP THE SINK WITH PUKE), HE COMES TO VISIT EVERY NOW AND THEN. I THINK HE'S A BIT JEALOUS OF MY NEW BOYFRIEND. HE'S A KANGAROO CALLED BOOGA. HE'S REALLY CUTE BUT HE DRESSES FOR SHIT.

I THINK HE WANTS TO MARRY ME.

PERVIS
PETER DUNCAN

THIS IS YOU

Hello mum!
xxx LOVE BOOGA. XXXX

WELL, YOU KNOW ME, I NEVER WANTED TO GET MARRIED, I ESPECIALLY DON'T WANT TO NOW, I MEAN I CAN'T. I MEAN, OH I'LL TELL YOU ABOUT THAT LATER.

ANYWAY, DO YOU REMEMBER THOSE TWO GIRLS WHO USED TO COME ROUND OUR HOUSE AFTER SUNDAY SCHOOL AND TRY ON YOUR UNDERWEAR? WELL THEY COME TO SEE ME QUITE A BIT. THE BORING ONE WITH BLACK HAIR FLIES A JET PLANE AND THE OTHER ONE (THE ONE YOU LIKED) DRIVES A SUBMARINE. WE'RE ALL TRYING TO GET A BASEBALL TEAM TOGETHER FOR NEXT SUMMER.

WELL, THAT'S ALL THE BORING STUFF. NOW, I'VE GOT SOME THINGS TO TELL YOU AND I DON'T WANT YOU GETTING ALL UPSET. AND I DON'T WANT

Doctor No

BOOGA AND ME ON BOOGA'S BIRTHDAY X

BOOGA GOES TO CHURCH!

TATOO I GOT DONE OUT THE BACK OF JUNKIES CAFE! (NEAT HA!?)

TEETH TEETH TEETH TEETH TEETH UNDERNEATH

YOU THINKING THAT YOUR DAUGHTER HAS GONE ALL WIERD AND SHIT.

BUT— DO YOU REMEMBER WHEN I WAS A KID AND YOU TOOK ME TO THAT FORTUNE-TELLER WOMAN AND SHE SAID THAT MY NAME MEANT 'THE RULE BREAKER' AND THAT I WOULD SOMEDAY BREAK ALL THE ESTABLISHED LAWS OF LIFE?

WELL MOM, IT WAS TRUE, IT'S HAPPENING! BUT I'M NOT JUST BREAKING RULES FOR THE SAKE OF IT, THERE SEEMS TO BE A REASON FOR EVERYTHING I DO. IT'S LIKE SOME KIND OF FORCE TAKING OVER MY LIFE.

I'M NOT SCARED OF THAT.

THERE ARE SO MANY STUPID PEOPLE, SO MANY STUPID LAWS. SHIT.

WHEN I GET TO SEE YOU NEXT I'LL EXPLAIN EXACTLY WHAT I'M ON ABOUT. BUT IT'S <u>BIG</u>!

ME AND SIS PLAYING BASEBALL IN THE BACK YARD. AGE 10 FOUND THIS ONE INSIDE THE SLEEVE OF MY NICK DRAKE ALBUM. THOUGHT YOU MIGHT WANT IT!

PERVIS   PETER'S TEETH   PETER DUNCAN

PEOPLE WORLD WIDE ARE LIVING A <u>LIE</u>. AND RUN THEIR LIVES AROUND A SYSTEM THAT IS COMPLETE <u>BOLLOCKS</u>.

ENCLOSED IS A SHORT NOTE THAT MUST BE GIVEN TO ONE OF MY FRIENDS IF ANYTHING SHOULD HAPPEN TO ME. THEY'LL KNOW WHAT IT MEANS.

I'D BETTER GO NOW, BEFORE BOOGA USES ALL THE SHOWER WATER. IT'S A HARD LIFE LIVING IN A TANK.

WELL, SO LONG MOM, HOPE TO SEE YOU SOON, LOVE, YOUR DAUGHTER,

TANK GIRL XXX

MY STUFFED KOALA YOU GAVE ME ON MY 15TH BIRTHDAY —(STUPID! GOT MY FINGER IN FRONT OF LENSE)

KEEP THIS SAFE

A POWERFUL LAVATORY CLEANER, THIS <u>WILL</u> WORK,
THE SIMPLEST EQUATION IN THE WORLD, THIS IS HOW IT WILL BE DONE.
I HERBY STATE—
THE SIMPLEST EQUATION.
EVERY ONE ALLOWED
THIS <u>WILL</u> WORK.   T.G.

P.S. THANKS FOR ALL THE WALNUTS AND TANGERINES
P.P.S. HOPE YOU LIKE ALL THE PHOTOS.

SATURDAY MORNING IN THE OUTBACK. GOD KNOWS HOW MUCH WE HAD TO DRINK LAST NIGHT. MY MOUTH FEELS LIKE I'VE BEEN EATING HANDFULS OF DRY CORNFLAKES AND I FORGOT TO SWALLOW. ...ANYWAY, AFTER PEELING MY FACE AWAY FROM BOOGA'S ARMPIT, IT WAS TIME TO ASK THAT PONDEROUS QUESTION OF ETERNAL LIFE...

...WHO'S TURN IS IT?...

BOOGA? COME ON BOOGA, IT'S NO USE PRETENDING YOU'RE ASLEEP YOU OLD BASTARD. YOU KNOW IT'S YOUR TURN!...

BUT I DON'T EVEN WANT ONE!

AND HOW COME IT'S NEVER TANK GIRL'S TURN?

YER BOOGA YOU WAISTOID! I DID IT LAST TIME YOU KNOW IT'S YOUR TURN!

LEAVE ME ALONE. I'M ASLEEP.

BECAUSE DEAR BOOGA, MY FINE WELL HUNG MARSUPIAL PLAYMATE, I ALWAYS BUY THE INGREDIENTS. AND BESIDES, I'M CRAP AT IT.

WELL, I GUESS I'D BETTER GO AND DO IT BEFORE THIS CONVERSATION PLUMS UNPLUMMED DEPTHS OF TEDIUM...

AND BEFORE I KICK YOU IN THE PLUMS!...

BOOGA'S TURN! (AGAIN)

I HATE MAKING THE PHUCKING TEA!

I LOVE TO START THE DAY WITH A DECENT CUP OF TEA, A GOOD HARD DUMP AND A SCRUB UP TO GET RID OF YESTERDAY'S MUCK AND SHIT...

MORNING STEVIE!

TWO SUGARS BOOGAAH!

"MY TANK IS JUST LIKE DOCTOR WHO'S TARDIS, ON THE OUTSIDE IT LOOKS REALLY SMALL AND INSIDE IT'S FULL OF SHIT!"

GALLERY: THIS MONTH WE SEE THE START OF OUR 'TAKE ART' GALLERY-SHOWCASING SOME OF OUR MORE TALENTED READERS WORK. LOOK, LEARN AND ENJOY. THESE ARE THE COMIC NERDS OF TOMORROW! ...

★ BY STEVEN WHORE FROM THE LAKE DISTRICT. PRIZE: PAM AYRES L.P.

★ PENELOPE PIPSTOP FROM SKEGNESS. PRIZE: DAY OUT FOR TWO IN WORTHING.

★ BY MICK MUDDLES FROM PORT SUNLIGHT. PRIZE: BEER TOKEN.

★ BY SPOCK O'KIRK FROM DURHAM. PRIZE: THE CRAP LAMPSHADE.

THANK YOU ALL FOR YOUR ENTRIES. WE ARE SORRY WE CAN'T RETURN THEM BUT THEY WERE ALL A LOAD OF SHIT.

"ONE VISION I SEE CLEAR AS LIFE BEFORE ME, THAT THE ANCIENT MOTHER HAS AWAKENED ONCE MORE, SITTING ON HER THRONE REJUVENATED, MORE GLORIOUS THAN EVER. PROCLAIM HER TO ALL THE WORLD WITH A VOICE OF PEACE AND BENEDICTION"......

I'M 23. LOOK AT ME, I'M 23

I CAN SEE YOU ALL FROM UP HERE..... ALL THE BOYS AND GIRLS.... ALL THE DICKS AND FANNYS.

AND WHAT OF THESE SEXUAL REVOLUTIONS, BOYS AND GIRLS?

ARE YOU IN THE RIGHT SEXUAL CATEGORY? THIS IS THE QUESTION.

WHO GIVES A SHIT....... TITS AND BALLS DICKS AND FANNYS.

GIVE ME THE CELIBATE VEGETARIANS FROM MARS ANYTIME.

I'D LOVE TO F*CK YOU UP.

I'D LOVE TO F*CK YOU UP.

SPEAKING OF DICKS, IT'S BOOG- AS BIRTHDAY TODAY....... I'D BETTER GET THE OLD TOSSER A PRESENT..

RIGHT! OFF TO DIRTY FRED'S OLD CURIOSITY SHOP...

VRIM! VRIM VRIM! VRIM! VRIM!

STORY: ALAN CHUCK MARTIN, ART: JAMIE TULIP, LETTERS: JAMIE, SOUNDTRACK: ABBEY ROAD, STUNT CO-ORDINATOR: STRETCH ARMSTRONG, DEADPOOL: THE BLOKE FROM THE RADION AUTOMATC ADVERT, THIS ONE FOR NICK, JAMIE © 1990

VRiiiiiMMM! -A

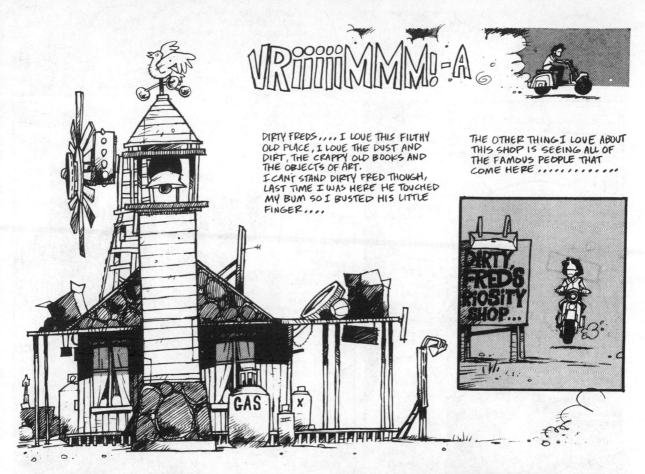

DIRTY FREDS.... I LOUE THIS FILTHY OLD PLACE. I LOUE THE DUST AND DIRT, THE CRAPPY OLD BOOKS AND THE OBJECTS OF ART.
I CANT STAND DIRTY FRED THOUGH, LAST TIME I WAS HERE HE TOUCHED MY BUM SO I BUSTED HIS LITTLE FINGER....

THE OTHER THING I LOVE ABOUT THIS SHOP IS SEEING ALL OF THE FAMOUS PEOPLE THAT COME HERE..............

AND ACCIDENTLY OVER-HEARING THEIR CONVERSATIONS....

IT IS WRITTEN THAT THE METEOR IS HALF THE SIZE OF THE MOON!....

AND IT'S COMING THROUGH OUR PART OF THE SOLAR SYSTEM IN THE NEXT TWENTY FOUR HOURS.... THE CHANCES ARE IT COULD HIT THE EARTH AND KILL US ALL!....

YUP!

JUST LIKE NOSTRADAMUS PREDICTED!

F-SURE

METEOR, EH? THAT GIVES ME A STARTLINGLY BRILLIANT IDEA!..

117

AND SO WITH THE METEOR STUCK FIRMLY ON TANK GIRLS BONCE BOOGA AND STEVIE CAN GET ON WITH THE BIRTHDAY CELEBRATIONS....

GEB BIS BUDDY BING OB BY HEAB!

STUPID, FAT COW!

I SAY STEVIE, DID BALLOON HEAD SAY SOMETHING?

WHO CARES.?! THAT METEOR STAYS ON HER SHOULDERS UNTIL WE'VE FINISHED WITH THIS SLAP UP FEED!

ANOTHER GALLON OF VINTAGE CIDER, MY DEAR BOOGA?

NOT FOR ME STEVIE, I'VE STILL GOT TO MAKE THE REST OF THOSE PHONE CALLS FOR TANK GIRL!

ABSOLUTE ASSHOLE ENDIN!

YOU WANKER BOOGA!....

PINTS OF VIEW:
CORRESPONDENCE WITH OUR FANS.....

PLANK GIRL
BY EARTHLET EARTH KIT
FROM MORECAMBE

DEAR JAMIE + ALAN
ON THE 4th OF DECEMBER 1989 I WAS LYING IN BED WITH REALLY SWOLLEN TESTICLES. SHORTLY, MY COPY OF DEADLINE Nº 14 WAS DELIVERED. AFTER READING THE ISH I SHOT MY LOAD ALL OVER THE LIVING ROOM CARPET,
YOURS, SPOCK O'KIRK
BOURNVILLE GRDN CITY

DEAR SPOCK,
CHEERS!
LOVE J+A

DEAR JAMIE AND ALAN,
I NOTICED THAT IN TANK GIRL #8 ON PAGE FIVE, FRAME 4, TANK GIRL IS WEARING A RING IN HER EAR, BUT IN THE NEXT FRAME SHE IS SPORTING A GROSS. HOW DO YOU EXPLAIN THIS DRASTIC MISTAKE?
BARRY HEADWOUND,
LITTLE-HAMPTON.

DEAR BARRY,
IF YOU EVER EVEN COME WITHIN TEN MILES OF OUR HOUSE WE WILL BREAK YOUR SHIT FILLED RETARDED SKULL, LOVE J+A

Dear Jamie and Alan,
Could we see again the scene from part two of the 'Australian Job' when Sub Girl grabs the burger. This is our most favorite ever,
Yours Hopefully,
The Chocolate Biscuit Club,
Chelmsford xxx

YOUR WISH IS OUR COMMAND!

EPITAPH.

NOT NEXT YEAR, NOT THE NEXT ONE,
NOT THE YEAR AFTER THAT. BUT AGES
FROM HERE,

CLAD IN LOVE STAINED SLEEPING BAGS,
DYING WITH FEET WRAPPED IN ENDLESS
SHIRTS AND PILLOW CASES,

CRUMBLING, WITH 99 FLAKES CLUTCHED
BETWEEN THUMB AND PALM, DRIPPING
YELLOW CREAM FROM TWIG FINGERS,
BASKING OUR WHITE HAIRED CHESTS ON
GREEN GRASSED PARKS UNDER PURPLE
SKIES. LAUGHING OVER COFFEE AFTER
BATH TUBS OF COFFEE HAVE PASSED
THROUGH OUR GUTS. HUDDLED, LONELY,
UNDER HEAPED CLOTHES, HERE LAY US ...

CUT AND DRESS

TANK GIRL*

STAND

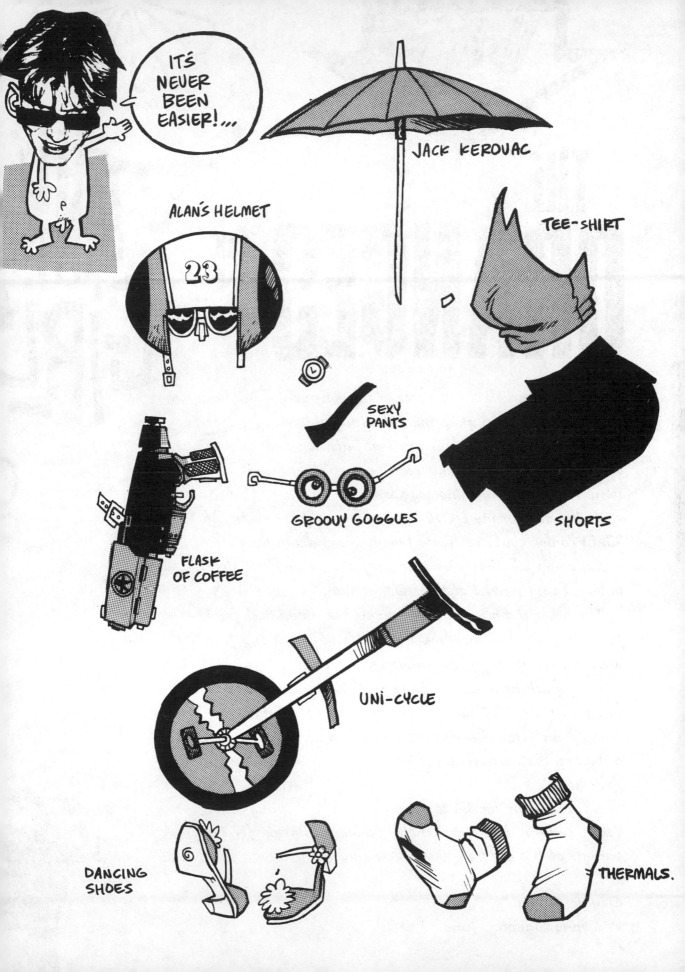

THE ORANGES OF TANK GIRL

It was an incredible day for comics. Looking very much like the peak of Beatlemania, the airport teamed with teenage boys and girls. some wearing strange hats, some completely bald (apart from a peculiar yellow clump at the front), and some wearing swimming goggles.

As the door of the DC10 opened, the majestic chorus of 'Get Wonky' could be heard twenty miles down the road.

Suddenly all was chaos as they took their first steps outward and waved at the eager crowd.

The police did a good job in holding the crowd back for a few minutes, but then the thousands of screaming fans were too much and the barriers were broken.

As a quick as a flash, Jamie and Alan turned tail and ran back inside the plane, which promptly took off.

Half an later the aircraft landed safely in a private airport on the south coast. The boys were quickly escorted to their hotel.

All good fun for those involved with this strange new youth culture, but I can't help, feeling distressed for the parents of the children who follow this odd craze.

George Jestical,
Worthing Gazette, June 1990

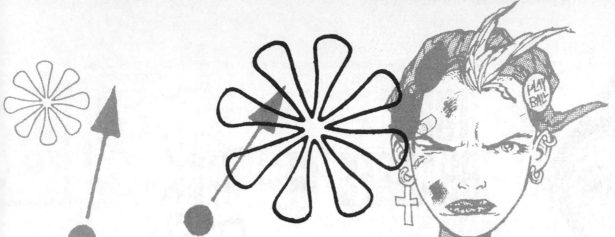

THE BIG BANG

For the longest time, I have had in my head the image of a sunset, viewed from a cattle ranch over dusty fields and orange mountains. This sunset was my childhood ideal.

In my twenty third year as a human being I am still able to recall this euphoric image, this all consuming feeling, as easily as turning on a television.

Around the time that this sunset first appeared in my thoughts (when I was five) I experienced an awakening that could only happen at so early an age.

As with most children around that time, I had in my possession a ridiculous 'toy' —

The hundred shot repeater cap gun.

No mother would hand her child a box of matches, but with this make—believe implement of death, I had the God given right to buy an unlimited supply of paper caps. This is my concern, the caps, not the gun.

Any person, who as a child, experienced the barbaric joy of thumping whole reels of paper caps with hammers, bricks or other heavy household objects, has experienced the awakening.

The familiar pungent smell, the electric flash and the Earth moving tremor of the blast shooting up your arm as you perform this primeval act, take your mind and spirit onto another plateau.

THE ORANGES OF TANK GIRL★

Recently, it has occurred to me that my ideal sunset is not actually an English sunset, or in fact an Earthly sunset at all, but a Martian sunset.

My theory is that everyone has a vague memory of this sunset, or of similar images, and that the feeling of well being that accompanies it.

These memories have been passed down generation to generation subliminally from our forefathers, via genes and through subconscious actions and rituals.

This way a form of reincarnation occurs and memories can be traced back to the birth of man in his present form.

Encoded into every episode of Tank Girl is a 'trigger' designed to provide a similar kind of awakening as the paper cap 'Big Bang'.

The feeling of well being, the memories of the distant past and the realization that all is not as it seems on this planet will follow naturally.

And in this way, we will help to speed up the evolution of Mankind.

Good and better

TEETH   TEETH

A DESIRE TO REACH THE TABLE TOP,

'WHO BUILT IT ?' ASKS THE CHILD,

AND RONNY DIGS HIS BIGGEST HOLE

IN THE DUSTY FIELD OUTSIDE.

TEETH.

A DESIRE TO DRAW A HOST OF GIRLS

MADE FROM ELONGATED CIRCLES,

'I FEEL LIKE A BOILED EGG.'

SAID THE ONE THAT STOOD OUT THE MOST,

'WE ARE THE OVAL-TEENS.'

SAID THE BUBBLE ABOVE THEIR HEADS,

TEETH TEETH

A DESIRE TO SMOKE MYSELF STERILE

WITH MENTHOL CIGARETTES,

TINY FINGERS REACH THE TABLE TOP,

'WHO BUILT IT ?' ASKS THE CHILD,

AND RONNY DIGS HIS BIGGEST HOLE

IN THE DUSTY FIELD OUTSIDE

To say that Jamie Hewlett is the most talented geezer in the whole world, ever, would be a crass and moronic understatement.

He is (and I quote) 'The Greatest'.

Jamie started drawing comics at the age of seven, whilst studying fine art at the Royal Academy.

He was heralded as the 'New Millias', but it was not to be.

At the age of seventeen he realised that the Academy was crap and left rather promptly, travelling to the South Coast to attend Worthing Art Collage.

Here he met up with the rather handsome comic artist, Mr Philip Bond, and the rather perplexed garibaldi fanatic, Mr Alan Martin.

Together the boys broke new ground in both Comics and Art with their rather splendid home made fanzine 'Atomtan'.

These days Jamie lives a reclusive life in a cellar near Worthing seafront.

A tall and dangerous shadow of his former self, he is often spotted riding his Chopper around the streets of sunny Worthing.

I BEAN STAND UP??

The release of 'Sugar Sugar' by The Archies in 1969 couldn't have come at a better time.

I can remember vividly the grinning face of young Alan and the wails of joy every time the record was played.

To the smiling three year old boy the tune came as an anthem, an anthem of the future !

Twenty years on and Alan is still whistling 'Sugar Sugar', using its subliminal influence to create such legendary stonkers as 'Ginsburg, Stipe and Kerouac', 'Hell City', 'Good Pictures', 'Mr Wonky' and of course the award winning 'Tank Girl'. All created with the brush of his genial friend and buddy, Jamie 'Jampot' Hewlett.

Good luck to him.

Jolly Jim,
The Bicycle King of Worthing.